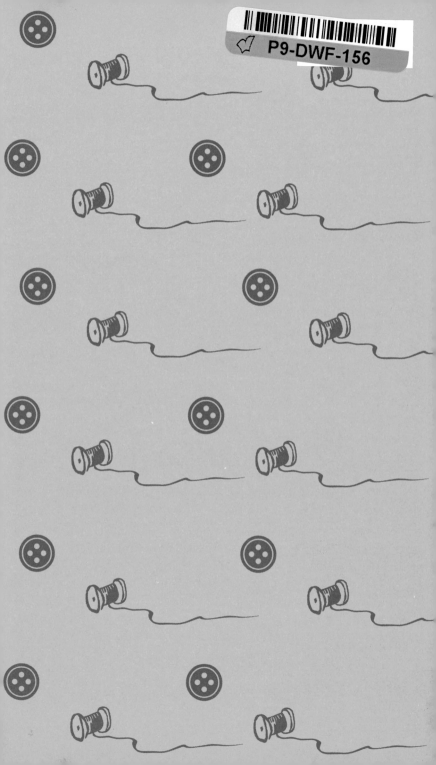

GRIN
and
BEAR
IT

The Wit & Wisdom of

CORDUROY

GRIN
and
BEAR
IT

The Wit & Wisdom of *CORDUROY*

Based on the characters created by *Don Freeman*

Pictures by Don Freeman and Jody Wheeler

VIKING

VIKING

Penguin Young Readers

An imprint of Penguin Random House LLC

375 Hudson Street

New York, New York 10014

First published in the United States of America by Viking,
an imprint of Penguin Random House LLC, 2018

ISBN 9780451479297

1 3 5 7 9 10 8 6 4 2

Manufactured in China   Set in Ionic MT
Book design by Nancy Brennan

BOOKS ABOUT CORDUROY

On your way to the top,
enjoy the ride.

Good friends
want what's best for you.
Pay attention to their advice.

To travel further, go together.

Curiosity didn't kill the bear....

You're never too small
to get where you need to go.

Love what you see
in the mirror.

There's no hurt so big that it can't be mended by friendship.

Remember, time-out
isn't forever.

Everybody needs a little
pick-me-up now and again.

Wherever you choose to go,
you're sure to find adventure.

No matter how nervous
you are, walk in like you
own the place.

Sometimes you have
to baby yourself.

If you've got something
to say, get on your soapbox
and say it!

Find your own style.

Step out of the shadows
and into the light.

A true friend always
has your back.

Sometimes you've just got
to go along for the ride.

You're never too grown-up
for a teddy bear.

Venture into the unknown.

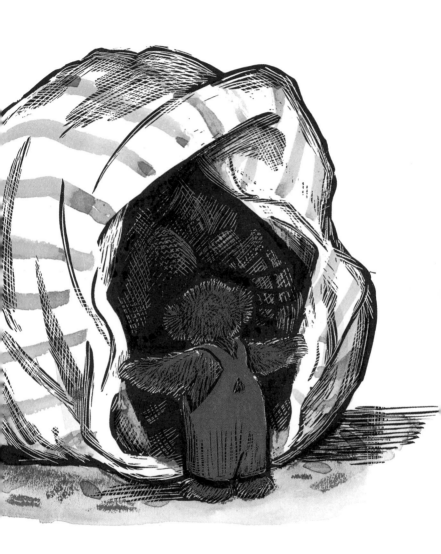

Friends come in all shapes, sizes, and species.

There's always a good
reason to party!

Better to get a big hat
than a big head.

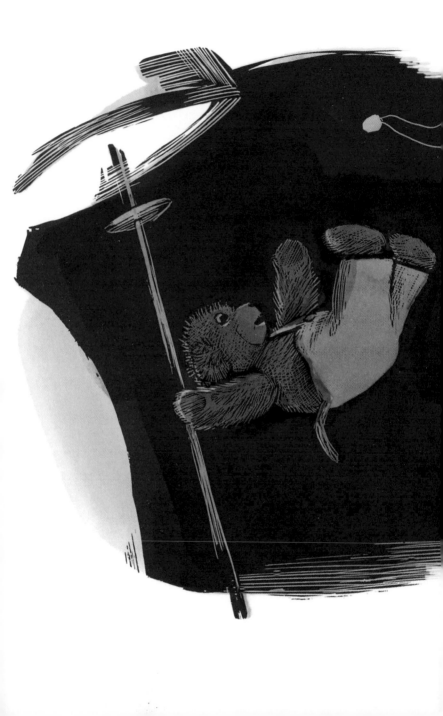

Sometimes you have to fall
so you know you're able
to get back up.

Make time for snuggling.

Nothing feels as good as
climbing into bed at the
end of a long day.

Never forget who you are—
and never forget who
loves you.